Edward T. D. Chambers

Quebec, Lake St. John

and the new route to the far famed Saguenay

Edward T. D. Chambers

Quebec, Lake St. John
and the new route to the far famed Saguenay

ISBN/EAN: 9783337351113

Printed in Europe, USA, Canada, Australia, Japan

Cover: Foto ©Andreas Hilbeck / pixelio.de

More available books at **www.hansebooks.com**

QUEBEC,

Lake St. John,

AND THE

NEW ROUTE TO THE
FAR-FAMED

SAGUENAY.

BY

E. T. D. CHAMBERS.

Quebec, Lake St. John,

···⊰ AND THE ⊱···

New Route to the Far=Famed Saguenay.

LAKE ST. JOHN, the mouth of the Saguenay, and the City of Quebec form the angles, upon the map of Canada, of an almost equilateral triangle, the three sides of which mark the route of the newest and grandest of Canadian summer tours. That portion of the trip represented by the base of the triangle and the lower half of its easterly side is famous wherever the praises of the Saguenay and the Lower St. Lawrence have been sung. Hitherto its only drawback has been the necessity of going twice over the same ground in one journey. Now all this has been changed. A few years ago the line of railway from Quebec to Lake St. John, which may be said to form the westerly side of the triangle, opened up to sportsmen the wildest woods and most plentifully stocked waters of the Canadian Adirondacks, and to tourists the far-famed yet mysterious Pikouagami, or Lake St. John, and its marvelous surroundings. Thousands of pleasure travelers, explorers, and anglers have taken advantage of the new railroad to visit the great inland sea and its mighty tributaries, and, like the visitors to the Saguenay, almost all of them returned by the way that they came.

There was a gap in the present triangular tour, extending from its northerly angle at Lake St. John to Chicoutimi, nearly half way down the easterly side of the triangle, which has only just been filled by the construction of the new railway extension, that renders the arrangements for the round trip complete, without the necessity of alternate *portages* and shooting of rapids for a distance of sixty to seventy miles. Now, well within the time heretofore occupied in making the Saguenay trip alone, tourists may visit by rail the far-famed Lake St. John, crossing the Laurentian Mountains, and passing the trout streams and lakes of the Canadian Adirondacks by the way; may sleep overnight and take dinner and breakfast at the magnificent Hotel Roberval, Lake St. John, and may continue, early next morning, by rail to Chicoutimi, and thence descend the Saguenay by steamer, and so return to Quebec by way of the St. Lawrence, or, perhaps, by Intercolonial Railway from River du Loup.

How this may be accomplished and what else may be done by sportsmen and tourists in the interesting country traversed by the new line of the far northerly Quebec & Lake St. John Railroad it is the province of the following pages to describe.

The tour commences and ends with

The City of Quebec,

the ancient capital of New France, the one "walled city of the North," — "the sentinel city that keeps the gates of the St. Lawrence," — and amongst all the cities of the New World, as Professor Roberts correctly puts it, "the grandest for situation, the most romantic in associations, the most distinctive and picturesque in details." "Quebec," says Joaquin Miller, "is the storehouse of American history, and the most glorious of cities,—beautiful, too, as a picture." She stands at the very threshold of this strong and impatient New World, in this age of progressive activity and enterprise, like a little patch of mediæval Europe, transplanted, it is true, upon a distant shore, but shutting out by her mural surroundings the influences that the whole of the surrounding continent has failed to exercise upon her. There is scarcely a foot here which is not historic ground, which is not consecrated, by well-established fact or tradition, to the memory of deeds of heroism, of instances of undying piety and faith, from the scene of Champlain's landing in the Lower Town to found his infant colony, to the world-renowned Plains of Abraham on the heights above, where Wolfe died to gain, and Montcalm shed his blood in the vain endeavor to save, the half of a continent.

"The earliest explorers of the far West, European heroes of martial strife and strategy and their dusky chieftain allies, noble matrons and self-sacrificing missionaries, whose doings live forever in the burning pages of Parkman, Lever, Charlevoix, and Casgrain, have left behind them here monuments of their zeal for the cause of religion and fatherland, or immortalized the ground which once they trod, the soil for which they fiercely contended, the spot where first they planted the symbol of their religion, or the dust which they reddened with their blood." Armed with a copy of the little guide-book from which the above extract is taken*, the tourist will find his stay in the Gibraltar of America far too brief to enable him to take in all the attractions of the city and its environs, its many historic localities, its churches and convents, its university, with its valuable collection of old paintings and well-equipped library and museum, and the many beautiful drives, and excursions, by rail and steamboat, to the Falls of Montmorency, Lorette, La Bonne Ste. Anne, Levis, New Liverpool, St. Joseph, and the Island of Orleans.

While taking in these and other attractions of the city and vicinity, the tourist may make his home in one of the most modern and most elegantly appointed hotels of the continent. Quebec's new hostelry, the Hotel Frontenac, commenced in 1892 and opened for the season of 1893, is due to the foresight and spirit of enterprise of the leading officials of the Canadian Pacific Railway. It occupies probably the finest hotel site in the world, on the far-famed Dufferin Terrace, under the shadow of the famous citadel, built by the Duke of Wellington, and yet from its high elevation overlooking the St. Lawrence and surrounding country for miles around, and stands where once stood the Chateau St. Louis, so famous in early Canadian history. It was erected by Champlain, the pious founder of Quebec, and later, was successfully defended against an English invasion by Count Frontenac, the French Governor, who, upon being summoned to surrender, told the messenger of the English Admiral to say that he would answer his summons by the mouths of his cannon. And he kept his word.

The St. Louis and the Florence are also well-known and much frequented hotels.

"All Aboard " for Lake St. John.

The through passenger trains for Lake St. John, to which handsome parlor cars are attached, leave the neat and pretty new depot of the Quebec & Lake St. John Railroad, on St. Andrew street, at 8.30 A. M. daily during the summer season, thus affording ample time for passengers arriving the same morning by the early trains

* Chambers' Guide to Quebec.

or the Montreal steamer, and desirous of making close connections, to take a bath and breakfast at their hotel before leaving for Lake St. John. Only a few hundred feet from the railway station is the splendid new iron bridge spanning the St. Charles river, 1,100 feet long, and which cost $200,000 to construct. Immediately over the bridge is Hedleyville Junction, whence the Quebec, Montmorency & Charlevoix Railway branches off to Montmorency Falls and La Bonne Ste. Anne. But our train has only paused for an instant at the Junction, and is already dashing up the slope of the nearest chain of the Laurentian Hills that bound the horizon as we look northward from the city in the direction of the Lake St. John country. No mountain region on the face of the globe offers more interesting features to the geologist than that of the Laurentides. This range forms the backbone of the oldest mountain chain upon the crust of our globe. Thousands of years before Noah's ark grounded upon the summit of Mount Ararat, or the fiat had gone forth which first shed created light upon a world of chaos, the mountains of which these Laurentian hills then formed 'the framework, lifted aloft their hoary heads, white with the snows of a thousand years. There are a number of indications of this condition of affairs which forbid any doubt on the subject. On the heights of Lorette, nine or ten miles from the City of Quebec, where the old discarded line of the Lake St. John Railway was cut through a heavy sand-bank, there were found pleistocene deposits of saxicava sand, containing astarte, saxicava-rugosa, and pecten-Greenlandica shells in great abundance. These are the self-same shells which are to-day found inhabited by living mollusks, in the cold, salt sea which washes the base of Greenland's icy mountains. In the glacial period of our planet's history there is no doubt that a similar cold, salt sea to that of Labrador and Greenland covered a great part of this Laurentian country to a height of many hundred feet above the present level of our own St. Lawrence.

Charlesbourg.

This typical and charmingly situated French-Canadian village is the summer residence of many of Quebec's citizens, who leave the city in the evening by the 5.30 local express, and return to business in the morning by the train that reaches Quebec at 8.40 A. M. There are two stopping places for trains in this village, one at Charlesbourg, three miles from the city, the other three miles farther on, at Charlesbourg West. The village, whose double-spired church and neatly whitened cottages and farmhouses are so

7

plainly seen from the heights of Quebec, standing on the slope of the receding hills, stretches all around and across between the two railway stations. The farming lands here traversed by the railway, and all those stretching away from the elevated plateau of Charlesbourg and Lorette back to the city of Quebec and into the intervening valley of the St. Charles, are amongst the most fertile in the Province. The best apples in the district are those grown upon the limestone grounds of this gently undulating country. A short distance above the church at Charlesbourg are still to be seen the ruins of the Chateau Bigot, the summer rendezvous of the shameless and profligate Intendant Bigot, the first great Canadian boodler, who, for his peculations at the expense of the then infant colony, was recalled to France, indicted, tried, and banished. In one of the secret passages of the old chateau was enacted the tragedy described in Kirby's entrancing historical romance, "The Golden Dog," which resulted in the violent death of Caroline, the unhappy Indian maid, at the instigation, so it is said, of her jealous rival, another favorite of the Intendant, no less a personage than the beautiful Angelique de Meloises, Madame Hugh de Péan, who is described as having imitated at Quebec, so far as she was able, the splendor and the guilt of La Pompadour, making the palace of Bigot as corrupt, if not as brilliant, as that of Versailles.

Lorette.

If the tourist has the time to spare, he will find it worth his while to give a day, or at least an afternoon, to visiting Lorette. He may leave the city by the 1.30 P. M. train, and return at 4.20 or 8.20. The station, which is eight miles from the city, is in the very middle of the Indian village, the home of the Christian Hurons, lineal descendants of those ancient warriors who waged such savage wars with the Iroquois in the time of Frontenac, two hundred years ago. These Indians gain their livelihood by hunting and trapping, and by the manufacture of snow-shoes, moccasins, toboggans, and fancy bead work. A visit to their homes is always interesting. Their chapel, which is over one hundred and fifty years old, is of the same model and the same dimensions as that of the Santa Casa, whence the image of the Virgin — a copy of that in the famous sanctuary — was sent to the Indians. The magnificent Falls of Lorette are alone well worth the journey to see. All the surroundings, where the foaming waters come tumbling down over rocks and stones and through picturesque gorges, are exceedingly wild. One can see the cascade by simply stepping aside from the roadway. But to be able to gaze upon the Falls in all their beauty, the tourist must descend the steps which lead to a ravine. Two minutes' walk will bring him to a moss-covered rock, where he may sit for hours listening to the noisy splash and watching the dashing waters as they hurry along, foaming and plunging over the stones. The Lorette Falls differ widely from the cataract of Montmorency, but they are just as striking in their way. Some think them even more beautiful. Just above the Indian village is the Chateau d'Eau, where, from a miniature lake formed by a dam across the river, two lines of iron pipe, one thirty and the other eighteen inches in diameter, draw off the water supply with which they serve the city of Quebec. From the heights of Lorette, as from those of Charlesbourg, and from the windows of the cars as the train rolls along the side of the hill, the view all around is of the most entrancing description. The city, in the distance, is bold and striking, rising up proudly out of the broad St. Lawrence, while the church spires, parliament buildings, and Laval University stand out grandly against the clear sky.

Four miles after leaving Indian Lorette, the train pauses a moment at Lorette Junction, and glides on to Valcartier, fourteen miles from Quebec, an agricultural settlement extending for many miles back from the railway, and which was originally settled largely by retired British officers and their descendants. No less than nineteen Waterloo veterans are buried in the cemetery here.

At eighteen miles from the city, immediately before pausing at St. Gabriel station, the train crosses

The Jacques Cartier River.

Here is afforded one of the prettiest views that can be seen from a car window anywhere. The river at this point is of considerable width. For several hundred feet above the bridge the fleecy water falls over a long-continued series of massive boulders, and, sixty feet below the railway, the seething fluid eddies around preparatory to its violent rush between the abutments of the bridge, only to peacefully rest, almost immediately afterwards, in the calm expanse of lake into which the river widens below the crossing of the railway. It is a somewhat dizzy scene, for the bridge is sixty feet above the water, but it is a substantial iron structure, and was built by the reliable firm of Clark, Reeves & Co., of Philadelphia. Notwithstanding its distance from the sea, the Jacques Cartier is a famous salmon river, whose praises have been sung by such well-known anglers as Charles Hallock, R. Nettle, Dr. Henry, Chas. Lanman, and others. Its name perpetuates the memory of the discoverer of Canada.

LAKE ST. JOSEPH.

St. Catherines is the next stopping place after St. Gabriel, and then, at twenty-four miles from Quebec, comes

Lake St. Joseph.

This beautiful sheet of water, which is only about an hour's ride from Quebec, has a crooked circumference of twenty miles, being eight miles long and from one to three in width. It is surrounded by mountains clad in magnificent hard-wood trees, reaching down to the water's edge, and embellished with many verdure-embowered nooks and oft-recurring vistas of charming scenery. In the middle of the lake the water is very deep and clear, and gently sloping beaches of hard sand render it most desirable as a bathing ground. A comfortable hotel, the Lake View House, and several summer cottages, have been constructed on the shores of the lake, and the pleasure steamer "Ida" makes frequent trips upon its waters. With all these advantages, it is not surprising that Lake St. Joseph should be rapidly becoming one of the most fashionable of Quebec's summer resorts. Its waters teem with various species of fish, chief amongst which are speckled trout, lake trout, black bass, and a white fish of excellent flavor to which the residents give the name of fresh-water shad. Brook trout grow very large in this lake, being sometimes captured in spring-time up to three pounds in weight. Bass are taken here most freely in the months of July and August, and the lake or fork-tailed trout, called by the French Canadians *touladi*, is caught throughout the entire season, either by trolling near the bottom of the deepest portions of the lake, or in fishing the same localities with live minnows. These forked-tail trout grow to an immense size, and have been known to exceed thirty pounds in weight.

Some five miles after leaving Lake St. Joseph station the railway runs for over two miles along the very brink of Lake Sergent, a placid but very beautiful body of water, the resort of perch and bass. Bourg Louis is the next station, and, at the thirty-sixth mile from Quebec, the train pulls up at

St. Raymond.

This is both the largest and the prettiest village between Quebec and Lake St. John on the main line of the railroad. The approach to it by railway from Quebec is very beautiful. It has been compared to a Swiss village in appearance, hemmed in, as it is all around, by mountains, along the side of one of which the train rushes down into the station, affording, on the way, a delightful panoramic view of the surrounding country from the car windows, looking towards the north. Through the village flows the interesting river St. Anne, and in the meadows along its banks, shaded by majestic elms, a short distance out of the village, are some of the most popular grounds for private picnic parties from the city. Various angling excursions may be made from St. Raymond to surrounding waters, and, at some few miles distance is the club-house of the Tourilli Fish and Game Club, situated on the opposite branch of the St. Anne River from the Little Saguenay. The club originally consisted of Quebecers only, but recently a number of American anglers have secured membership in it. Some of the trout taken by members of this club are exceedingly heavy.

Allen's Mill and Perthuis are the next stations, and at neither of these localities, nor yet at many another along the road at which the train stops, was there the slightest sign of settlement before the construction of the railway through these then forest solitudes. The same remark is applicable to

Rivière à Pierre,

fifty-eight miles from Quebec, where excellent agricultural ground abounds, and where quite a number of settlers have already taken up land. Near the station is the junction of the Lower Laurentian Railway with the Quebec & Lake St. John. The Lower Laurentian runs through a country famous for the fishing to be had in its waters, and for the hunting in its woods. Caribou and partridges are reported plentiful here in winter. The road runs in a westerly direction from Rivière à Pierre Junction, while the Quebec & Lake St. John continues on towards the north. At present the Lower Laurentian runs to St. Tite Junction, north of Three Rivers, where passengers for the latter city connect with the Piles branch of the C. P. R. It traverses not only a splendid sporting country, but several fine agricultural parishes and rich timber lands, and is destined, it is hoped, in the not far distant future, to form a link in an important line of railway connecting Quebec with Parry Sound on Georgian Bay, which would become the natural and by far the shortest existing outlet for the wheat of the great West, that is now conveyed as far as Duluth by the western roads of the United States, and thence finds its way to Eastern seaports by a comparatively long and expensive route.

Fishing Clubs.

Shortly after passing Rivière à Pierre Junction, and proceeding northward along the line of the Quebec & Lake St. John R. R.,

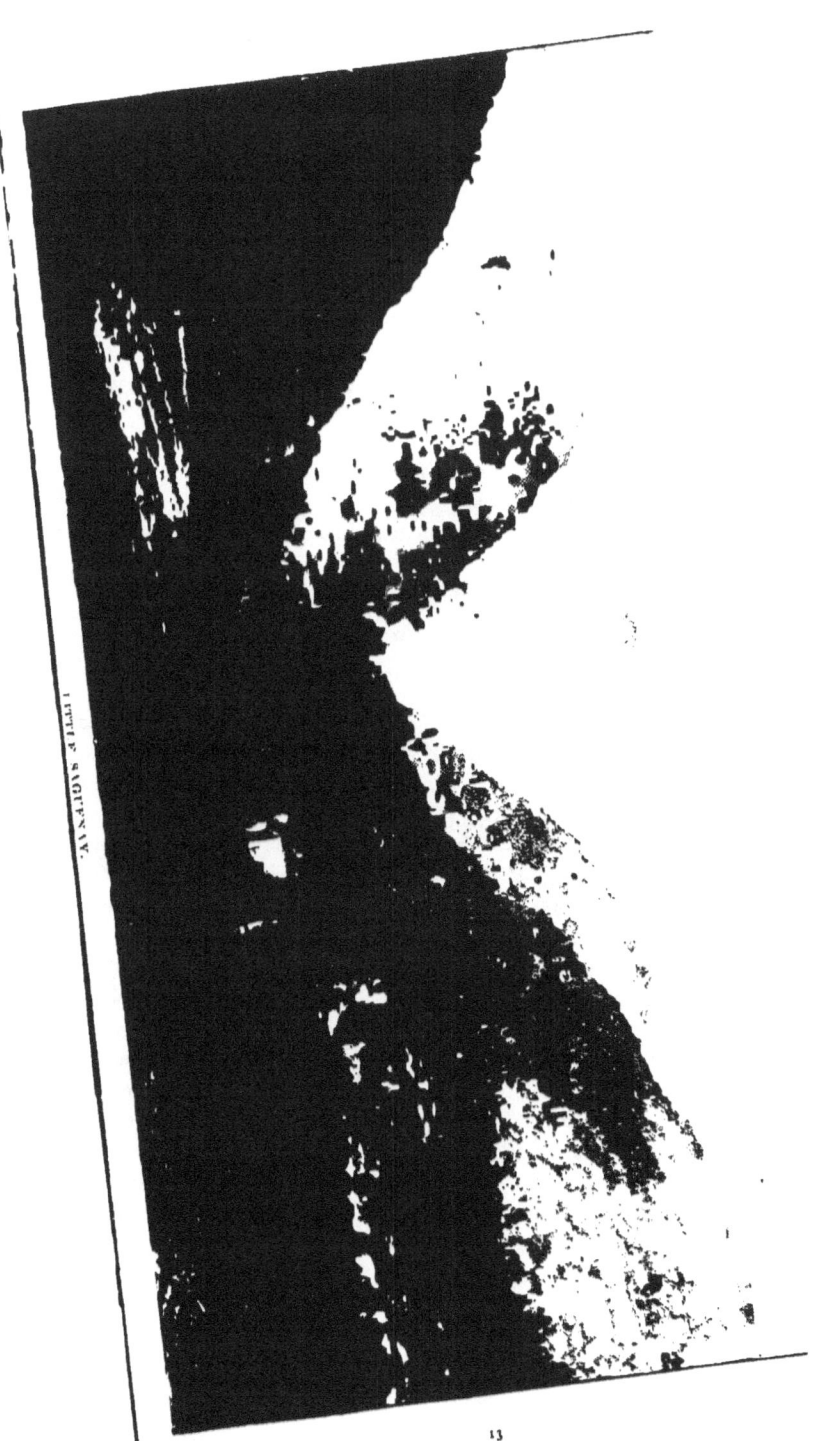

LITTLE RIGLAVIK.

the tourist finds himself in the midst of the great fish and game preserves of this delightfully wild country. Thick woods fringe the sides of the railway track, and here in winter both white and Indian hunters track the caribou. The whole of this territory is a perfect network of rivers and lakes, all of which literally swarm with fish. Numerous clubs have been formed to lease the fishing rights in certain portions of these waters, almost all of which have erected handsome club-houses at their respective headquarters. Some of them control at least ten square miles of territory, including often no less than scores of lakes, nearly all connected, or at the best only separated by country that is easily portaged. Two of the largest and most important Quebec clubs owning fishing preserves in this district are the Laurentides, whose club-house is seventy miles from Quebec, and not far from the railway, and the Stadacona, ninety-four miles from the city, with headquarters in sight of the car windows.

Before reaching these club lakes, however, the railway commences to skirt along the bank of one of the largest and most beautiful of the many magnificent trout streams of this section of the country. This is

The Batiscan River.

Its course is followed by the railway for between twenty and thirty miles. It is generally here from one hundred to four hundred feet in width, running frequently through such narrow mountain passes as barely to leave room for the railway track on one of its shores. It is a succession for the most part of wild, leaping cascades, and dashing, foaming rapids, with occasional stretches of deep, dark water that contrast strangely with the rough and rocky descents that form the chief characteristics of the river's course through this wild, mountainous country. The beauty of the scenery all along this Batiscan valley must be seen to be appreciated, and none who have observed it can ever forget its wild grandeur. The peculiarly bold abruptness of the mountains in this part of the country will also attract the attention of the observant tourist. All the lakes that are drained into the Batiscan contain immense quantities of speckled trout. The author of a paper in *Outing*, entitled "Along the Upper Batiscan," Mr. George R. Mosle, writes: "The sport here during a stay of fifteen days exceeded anything I have known, whether in the famous Moosehead region of Maine, or among the thousand lakes in the peninsula of Northern Michigan and Wisconsin. After the nrst day we decided to throw back all trout weighing less than one pound, and even then found we had a good many to spare at the close of a day's fishing. The largest trout captured by our party was a beauty of five and a quarter pounds. . . . The next largest weighed four and a half pounds. Besides these two largest we got a number over two and three pounds,—one catch of ten trout weighing eighteen pounds, and one of seven weighing sixteen and a half pounds."

At a distance of 113 miles from Quebec is

Lake Edward,

the largest body of water between the St. Lawrence and Lake St. John. Its original and more appropriate name is Lac des Grandes Isles, for in its length of twenty miles are numerous islands, large and small, all beautifully wooded, and often rising to a considerable height out of the water. The shores of the lake are also luxuriously wooded to the very edge of the water. A more picturesque lake it would be impossible to find anywhere. Its waters are so delightfully pure, cold, and clear, that not only is it a treat to drink them in the warmest weather, but upon clear days, the reflection of its richly timbered shores and islands is mirrored in the surface as in a glass, and the angler may quite often distinguish distinctly the bottom of the lake at a depth of ten to twenty feet. In these deep pools, some of which are continually cooled by the upward bubbling of fresh-water springs, there love to linger in refreshing indolence those monster trout,— handsome red-bellied specimens of the true *salmo fontinalis,*— weighing often from four to six pounds each, which have made this lake so famous. Marvelous stories have been written of how voraciously these speckled beauties take the fly in the summer season, and that they are plentifully captured with bait there is not the slightest matter of doubt. The best fly fishing in the summer season about this lake has been found by the present writer in the *Rivière au Rats,* one of the lake's feeders that enters it from the West. Here, however, the trout are not nearly so large as in the body of the lake. In August and September two to four pound trout rise readily to the fly in the River Jeannotte, the outlet of Lake Edward, permission to fish which must be obtained from the Orleans Fishing Club of Quebec, the lessees of the rights. In the lake itself, on the contrary, the fishing is free to all patrons of the railway,—the Company leasing it for their benefit from the Provincial government. There is an excellent hotel at the railway station, which is on the very edge of the lake, kept by Mr. J. W. Baker, where boats, camp outfits, and guides can always be obtained.

LAKE EDWARD.

There are also facilities for camping out on the shores of the lake, as Adirondack Murray, Kit Clarke, and C. H. Farnham of

Harper's Magazine have already done for weeks at a time. These brilliant writers have all sung the praises of Lac des Grandes Isles, to a recital of whose attractions Mr. Clarke has devoted no inconsiderable space in his charming little booklet entitled " Where the Trout hide." He says : —

" Beneath the umbrageous protection of majestic forests, hidden deep in the sheltered recess of a trackless wilderness, bordered completely by pompous wood-crowned mountains, reposes in peaceful seclusion Lac des Grandes Isles. Imperial domes of mutable green rear their reverential crests above its incurvated shores, and no sound breaks the stately silence of the tremendous solitude save the chirrup of the wild birds, or the measureless sigh of the winds among the unblazened trees. Its soft, rippling waters bathe the golden sand-shores in undulating swells, while, anon, huge boulders raise their titanic dimensions in capricious and grotesque outlines. Every vision is a spectacle of surpassing beauty. Bent, curved, and oddly distorted, its twenty miles of longitude encompass a hundred miles of shore, while many of its crooked bays, penetrating deep between the lofty hills, are as yet absolutely an undiscovered bourne into which no chivalrous civilized creature has ever ventured. Rich odors of balsam, spruce, and cedar encumber the cloudless atmosphere with a delicious fragrance, and every breath of the balmy air is invigorating and strengthening beyond description.

"Gemmed with numberless irregular and quaint islands, some of miles in length and others but the fragment of an acre in extent, the oarsman becomes entangled amid their intricate and puzzling watery ways, and, unless guided by subtle discretion, he is lost in a labyrinth of wondrous beauty.

" The trout of Lake Edward are exceedingly brilliant in color, much more variegated than the ordinary fish of the species, and in size have been taken approximating five pounds in weight, while still larger specimens have been seen time and again. The numbers of trout wrested from these waters almost surpass belief, yet they are not absolutely crazy, and will not frantically seize the decoy at any and every opportunity. Among all fish the trout is most conceited, contumacious, and pig-headed. When he won't, he won't, and there's an end on't. Great big fellows can be seen in the clear water, moving about carelessly and lazily, tantalizing the angler as he sits in his boat, vainly offering every inducement to tempt the fish into a breach of reserve."

Kit Clarke's camp is now the rendezvous of the Paradise Fin and Feather Club, whose president is Judge Henry A. Gildersleeve of New York, and which counts upon its list of members the names of President Cleveland, ex-Mayor Grant of New York City, C. B. Jefferson, H. C. Miner, John C. Davis, Dr. E. R. Lewis, Dr. William F. Duncan, and several other anglers of note.

The Height of Land.

A hundred and twenty-six miles from Quebec, or thirteen beyond Lake Edward, the height of land is reached, and the streams along the side of the railway are henceforth seen to flow northwards in the direction of Lake St. John, instead of southwards towards the St. Lawrence, as did those on the other side of the watershed. This summit is 1,500 feet above the level of the St. Lawrence, and 1,200 above that of Lake St. John. There is a perceptible increase, too, in the rate of speed attained by the train, as compared with the time that was made on the heavy up grades. Within the last few years both these grades and the principle curves upon the line have been considerably improved, at a cost of something like a million of dollars. Notwithstanding the present excellence of the road-bed, there is excitement enough, in all conscience, in the journey through the wild mountain region here traversed by the railway. In places the road has been cut through solid rocks of gneiss, granite, or hornblende, and splendid granite quarries are now being worked in the vicinity of both Miquick and Rivière à Pierre stations. There are some localities where it has been found necessary to build up lofty embankments for the road-bed, and in others the railway hugs the side of a mountain as it runs nearly half way around it, while on the off side of the track is a precipitous gorge hundreds of feet deep, down which the tourist may gaze far over the tops of the highest trees. Notwithstanding these obstacles of nature, the railway has been constructed in the most solid manner; its wide, well-ballasted embankments, heavy steel rails, smooth track, and excellent equipment of new rolling stock, from the best car-building establishments in America, making it one of the safest and most comfortable lines that it is possible to travel upon.

The preserves of a number of American fishing clubs are situated near the line of the railway, between Lake Edward and Lake St. John.

Lake Kiskisink.

Cedar Lake, or more correctly Kiskisink, is the first stopping place for the train after leaving Lake Edward. It is 135 miles from Quebec. Here are the holiday headquarters of the Metabetchouan Fishing and Game Club, which counts in its membership quite a number of New England millionaires. These gentlemen have a handsome club-house alongside the railway station at Kiskisink, on the margin of the lake of that name,— a beautiful sheet of water nine miles long,— and also fish the famous Bostonnais River, the outlet of Kiskisink, where large speckled beauties constantly rise to the anglers' flies from early spring to the very close of the season at the end of September. In addition to these waters the Club controls the fishing in the central portion of the Metabetchouan. Its president is U. S. Senator O. H. Platt, of Meriden, Conn.

Twenty-eight miles of the upper portion of the Metabetchouan are leased by the Philadelphia Fishing and Game Club, of which Amos R. Little, Director of the Pennsylvania Railroad, is president, while the lower part of the same river for some fifteen or twenty miles, and excepting some ten miles from its mouth, is fished exclusively by the Amabalish Fish and Game Club, of Springfield, Mass. E. S. Brewer is president of this club, and D. N. Coats vice-president, and some of the finest trout ever taken out of Canadian waters have come from the lakes and streams which it controls. The club-house is some distance back from the railway, and is usually reached by driving from Chambord Junction.

Lac Gros Visons and Lake Bouchette

are both seen from the train, and both are well worth seeing, especially Lake Bouchette, which is an exceedingly beautiful body of water, lying away in a partially cleared valley a little to the west of the railroad. The station at the lake is 160 miles from Quebec, and here the members of the newly formed club of New Haven fishermen disembark from the train to reach their preserves, which include the famous Lac des Commissaires and all tributary waters. An immense catch of speckled trout was taken here by members of the club in September, 1892, several of their fish weighing from two to four pounds each.

The fishing of the river Ouiatchouan, which flows out of Lake Bouchette towards Lake St. John, is leased to a club of gentlemen

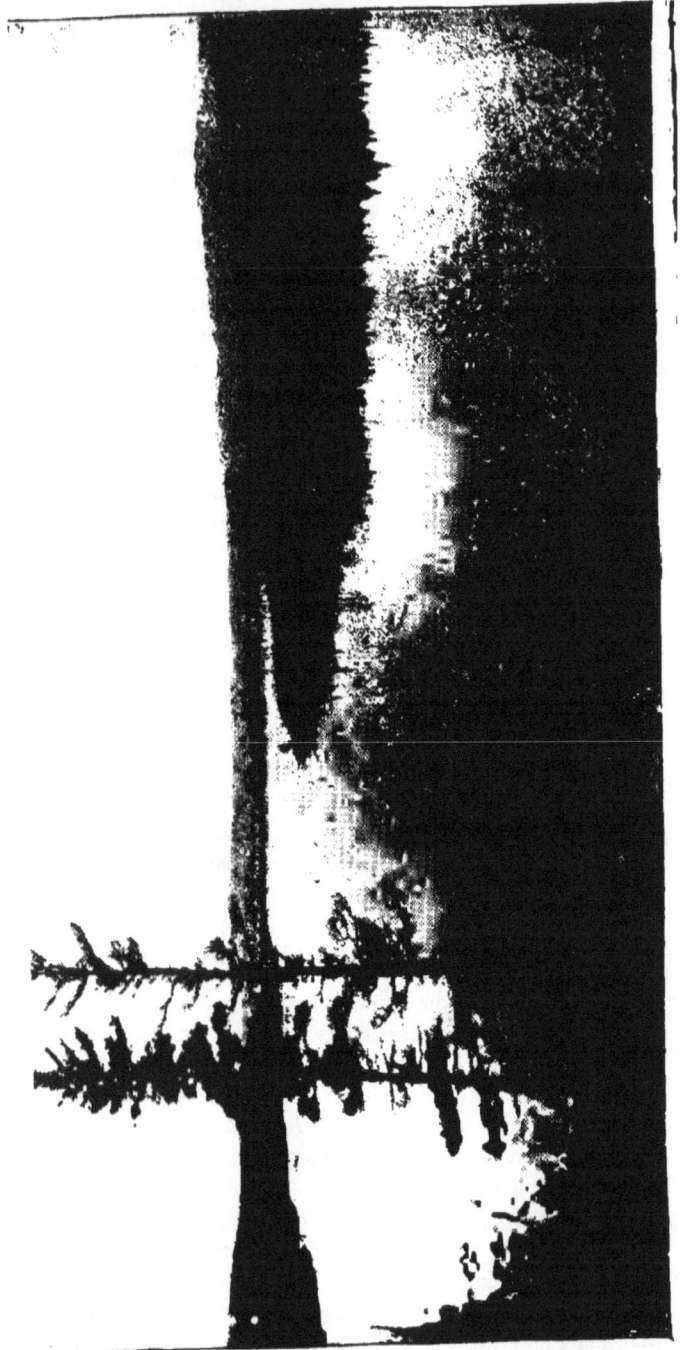

belonging to Roberval, Lake St. John. The late Dr. Lundy, of Philadelphia, and Mr. Eugene McCarthy, of Syracuse, who obtained permission to fish this stream in August, 1892, took out of it an enormous number of very heavy trout.

From this point onwards to Lake St. John the signs of settlement grow more frequent, and the tourist may at short intervals notice the humble beginning of new settlers, attracted here by the railway, who are gradually building themselves homes and clearing farms in what was a few years ago nothing but primeval forest.

Dablon

is reached four miles past Lake Bouchette, and is quite a new parish, possessing but little interest for the tourist excepting such as attaches to its name, which it has received for the purpose of perpetuating amongst the people of this country the memory of the Jesuit Father, Claude Dablon, who, in company with Father Druillettes, went, in 1661, as far as Lake Nikouban, at the head of the Ashuapmouchouan river, where a great trading fair was held annually by the Indians. The *Relations des Jesuites* speak of the journey as "the first voyage made toward the Northern Sea."

De Quen.

This is the name of the station immediately north of Dablon, at a distance of six miles. It has been named after the discoverer of Lake St. John, Father Jean De Quen, who, with Father Lallement (subsequently martyred by the Indians), established the old Jesuit College at Quebec. It was in 1647 that De Quen discovered Lake St. John. The Indian converts that he had made at Tadousac had carried the tidings of Christianity to Lake St. John in advance of the missionary's visit, but learning that some of them were ill and very much desired to see him, he braved the difficulties of the journey by way of the Saguenay river and the subsequent mountain portages to avoid the rapids of the Grand Discharge, and was the first white man to set foot upon the shores of the inland sea. How marvelously exact is his description of Pikouagami, as the Indians called the great lake, may be judged from the following extract: "This lake is so large that it is difficult to see the opposite shores. It appears to be of a round shape; it is deep, and swarming with fish. Pike, perch, salmon, trout, doré, whitefish, carp, and several other kinds, are caught in it. It is surrounded by a flat country, terminated by high mountains at a distance of three, four, or five leagues from its shores. It is fed by the waters of about fifteen rivers, which serve as highways to the different little nations that live in the lands whence they flow, by means of which they come to fish in the lake, and to interchange articles of commerce and friendship with each other."

Chambord Junction,

situated in the midst of a settlement overlooking Lake St. John, and named after the royal house of old France, is 177 miles from Quebec, and the next station to De Quen. Here the railway divides into two branches, one running to the east along the southerly shore of the lake, and thence to the head of navigation upon the Saguenay at Chicoutimi. The length of this division is fifty-one miles. That which runs to the west follows the shore of the lake until about half way up its westerly side, at the Roberval Hotel, which is fourteen miles from Chambord, and the head-quarters of all tourists and anglers desirous of fishing the lake, any of its tributaries, or the Grand Discharge, or of remaining for some time in this charming country. Even tourists who are simply taking the round trip should dine and sleep upon the night of their arrival at the Hotel Roberval, as by branching off to the east from Chambord Junction they will not only be deprived of the finest views of Lake St. John and the surrounding country, but will also miss seeing

The Ouiatchouan Falls,

one of the most picturesque bits of scenery in these northern wilds, where the waters of the Ouiatchouan, the outlet of Lake Bouchette, leap over a rocky precipice to near the level of the lake, not far from its southwest angle. The Falls are 236 feet in height, and rival in altitude those of Montmorency, while they far surpass them in the distribution of their waters, as they are lashed into foam by the projecting rocks. "Ouiatchouan" in the Montagnais dialect means "Do you see the falls there?" The beautiful Ouiatchouan Falls may be seen for many miles around, and from every part of the lake, and have given to the river its name. A fine view of their upper portion may be had from the car window as the train rushes along between them and the lake. Just above the railway bridge that spans the mouth of the river, its waters spread out into a majestic pool, in which the spring-time fishing for ouananiche or fresh-water salmon is at its very best from about the 20th of May to the 15th or 20th of June. There is a railway station at Ouiatchouan, and it is a pleasant drive of six miles to it from Hotel Roberval. There is a good

OUIATCHOUAN FALLS.

23

footpath in from the roadway to the very foot of the falls, and
heavy trout are sometimes taken there. The footpath route
affords the tourist some splendid views of the narrow gorge
through which the boiling waters of the Ouiatchouan rush toward
the lake, making a variety of scenes, quite as exciting as those
witnessed at the far-famed Natural Steps above the Falls of

HOTEL ROBERVAL.

Montmorency. A few minutes' ride on the cars from Ouiatchouan
brings the tourist to the end of the first stage of his journey,—
the modern and elegantly equipped

Hotel Roberval,

immediately before reaching which the train crosses the wildly
playful Ouiatchouaniche or Little Ouiatchouan, which rushes into

the lake over a rocky and rough descent, where its waters are lashed into spray as they sportively leap in cascade or dash onward in a succession of picturesque rapids.

Roberval is a name famous in Canadian history, being that of a French governor sent out to New France more than three and a half centuries ago, whose mission, however, ended in disaster, while he himself is said by some authorities to have been finally massacred in Paris, while others assert that he never returned from his last voyage up the Saguenay. The hotel Roberval is a handsome building overlooking the lake, and close to both the steamboat landing and the hotel station of the railway. It has accommodation for three hundred guests, and is one of the most commodious as well as one of the most comfortable houses in Canada. It is supplied with billiard room, bowling alley, and a promenade, ball, and concert hall, and its dining hall measures seventy by thirty-five feet. The furnishings are all quite new and exceedingly handsome, and the house is supplied with hot and cold water and with electric light and bells throughout, even the grounds surrounding it being illuminated by electricity at night. The outdoor attractions are lawn tennis, croquet, fishing, bathing, boating, and driving. The view of

Lake St. John

from the windows of the hotel is quite sea-like, and, even in the clearest weather, the vision can scarcely reach to the opposite shore at the Grand Discharge, a distance of some twenty-five miles. The inland sea is almost circular in shape, being some eighty-five miles in circumference. It is fed by a number of very large rivers, which Mr. Murray declares are well worthy of a volume to themselves, and most of which bear musical Indian names, while all of them swarm with fish. There is, first of all, the Peribonca, or "Curious River," over four hundred miles long; the Mistassini, or "River of the Big Rock," over three hundred miles in length, and nearly two miles wide at its mouth ; the Ashuapmouchouan, or "River where they Hunt the Moose," from two hundred and fifty to three hundred miles long. all flowing in from the north and northwest; the Ouiatchouan and Ouiatchouaniche, which have been already described, and the Metabetchouan, flowing from the south.

Scene among the Islands

Grand Discharge

Perfected Rapids Gt. Falls

View from Signal-Rock

Island House

Landing at Island House

View from the Island

Scene of Grand Discharge

Steamers

leave the hotel as required, to carry tourists into the mouths of these rivers, and those who desire to ascend them in birch-bark

Mistassini River

canoes may find guides, canoes, camping outfits, supplies, fishing tackle, etc., at the Hotel Roberval, before starting.

In the months of May and June excellent ouananiche fishing may be had in the lake, immediately in front of the hotel. From about the end of

View from 1st Island

June this fishing is good in the Grand Discharge, whither the steamer "Mistassini" crosses daily, from Hotel Roberval to the Island House, a hostelry built on an island of the Discharge, in the midst of the most magnificent scenery, specially

Island House

for the accommodation of anglers and tourists. It is also well supplied with guides and canoes, is under the same management as the Hotel Roberval, and has accommodation for nearly a hundred guests. The "Mistassini" is a perfectly new, steel-framed boat, staunch and fleet, and capable of accommodating four hundred passengers. It is admirably furnished and equipped with everything necessary for the comfort of passengers, and especially of that of the ladies. Her captain claims that he would be quite ready to cross the Atlantic in her. The steamers "Peribonca" and "Undine" are available for excursions to other parts of the lake.

Ouananiche Fishing.

Experienced anglers declare that no other fresh-water fish, excepting perhaps the salmon, afford so much sport to the fly fisherman as the ouananiche. Anglers and others desirous of learning more about this famous fish, which has the habit of making such extraordinary leaps when impaled on a fly-hook, that it fights nearly as much in the air as in the water, should address a postal card to the Tourist Department of the Quebec & Lake St. John Railway, asking for a copy of the illustrated guide to the " Haunts of the Ouananiche." Meanwhile it may be said that this extraordinary fish, which is peculiar to Lake St. John and its tributary waters, is really a fresh-water salmon, and that by some epicures its flesh is considered superior to that of the true *salmo salar.* Its name is Indian, and signifies "little salmon," for "*iche*" in the Montagnais dialect is a diminutive, and "*ouanan* " means "salmon." Anglers from all parts of the United States, even from as far south as Texas, visit Lake St. John and its tributaries and the Grand Discharge to enjoy the sport of fighting and killing the ouananiche, and, in 1892, Captain and the Lady Cecilia Rose, Colonel Andrew Haggard, a brother of the famous novelist, Monsieur and Madame Petit of Paris, and other distinguished Europeans, crossed the Atlantic for the express purpose of whipping these celebrated waters.

To the north of the lake, twenty miles up the Mistassini, is a newly established

Trappist Monastery,

founded in 1892, and occupied by some of "the silent monks of Oka," of which curious order a most interesting description appeared in the *Cosmopolitan* for December, 1892. The monks of this order were expelled from France in 1880. They lead the most austere lives, eat and drink nothing but bread, vegetables, and water, rise at two o'clock every morning, lash their bodies with a whip every Friday, devote their whole time to farm labor and their devotional exercises, and never speak to each other except to utter the salutatory warning, "*Memento mori*" (" Remember death "). All business is transacted and all orders given by a foreman or director of work.

At Pointe Bleue, only three miles distant from the Hotel Roberval, on the lake shore, are the reserve and village of

The Montagnais Indians,

who, in winter, hunt and trap the woods lying between Lake St. John and Hudson's Bay. These Indians are well worth a visit. They are amongst the most interesting of the North American aborigines, and are exceedingly dark of skin. The furs that they

collect in winter, and that form their principal means of subsist-
ence, are exchanged by them with the factors of the Hudson's
Bay Company for the ordinary necessaries of life. Very often, if
game is scarce in the winter season, they suffer the pangs of
hunger, and members of the tribe have been known to die in the
woods of starvation. The squaws display great admiration for
gay colors, and wrap their shoulders in the brightest of bright
cotton handkerchiefs, which are also used as head-dresses for the
girls. The costume of a Montagnais matron is incomplete without
the tribal tuque, similar in shape to the ordinary tuques of

MONTAGNAIS INDIANS.

Canadian snow-shoers, but with the point caught down in front to
the band, and the whole formed of alternate pointed stripes of
red and black, each stripe piped in blue. It is exceedingly interesting, when they are home from the woods in the summer season.
to hear them sing in their church, in their own peculiar language,
in adoration of the Virgin. Some few of them, however, are
Protestants, having been baptized at the English mission at
Moose Factory, Hudson's Bay. These have a little church of
their own.

   Mr. W. H. H. (Adirondack) Murray, in speaking of the Montagnais Indians of Lake St. John, says:—

"They are the 'Mountaineers' of ancient times and wars, and dwelt among the Laurentian Hills. They were a brave stock, and they and the Esquimaux of Labrador were never at peace. The Mounds of Mamelons at the mouth of the Saguenay could tell of wars fought on them for a thousand years, could their sands but speak. The Montagnais at Roberval are great hunters, skilled trappers, great canoemen and runners. They are a racial curiosity, and worthy of study on the part of the intelligent tourist, and the sight of them, and their peculiarities will be entertaining to all."

In the summer season they are ready to act as guides for tourists and anglers, and excellent guides they are, too. They may often, when not otherwise engaged, be found busy building birch-bark canoes, and every step of their process illustrates the marvelous exactness of Longfellow's noted description in "Hiawatha.' Wonderful indeed are the architecture and mechanism of these *"cheemauns";* so light and swift, with their pointed bows, and walls of birch bark, sewn together with the fibrous roots of the larch or tamarack; so stout and strong, with their framework and ribs of cedar boughs; so close and dry, with their seams securely closed with "the balm . . . the tears of balsam, and the resin of the fir tree."

> " Thus the birch canoe was builded
> In the valley, by the river,
> In the bosom of the forest;
> And the forest's life was in it,
> All its mystery and its magic,
> All the lightness of the birch tree,
> All the toughness of the cedar,
> All the larch's supple sinews;
> And it floated on the river
> Like a yellow leaf in autumn,
> Like a yellow water-lily."

The family of the Montagnais was formerly divided into various tribes, such as the Tadoussaciens, who hunted the lower part of the Saguenay country; the Chekoutimiens, farther to the west, who took their name from Chicoutimi, as the Tadoussaciens did their's from Tadousac; the Piegouagamiens, who hunted the shores of Pikouagami, or Flat Lake, as they called Lake St. John; the Mistassins, whose hunting-grounds lay to the north, between Lake St. John and Lake Mistassini; the Chemouchouanistes, who trapped and hunted the valley of the Ashuapmouchouan, and the Nekoubanistes, a tribe hailing from the extreme northwest of the Lake St. John country round about Lake Nekouban, one of the sources of the great river that may be considered as the commencement of the Saguenay, and that is quite as far from Lake St. John as the latter is from Quebec.

Hunting the moose, the caribou, the bear, and other large game, is attended with great success in the woods surrounding Lake St. John, while partridges, ducks, and geese are abundant in their season. The number of the geese supplied by the Indians at Fort Albany, James Bay, to the Hudson Bay Company is 36,000 annually, so that some idea may be formed of the number that fly southwards over Lake St. John every autumn.

Roberval to Chicoutimi.

The railway trip from the Hotel Roberval to Chicoutimi, the headquarters of navigation on the Saguenay, is the most novel, one of the most interesting, and the most recently opened up link in the entire round trip. The scenery that it offers is of the most varied and beautiful description. The distance between the two points is sixty-four miles, which is run in about two hours, thanks to the admirable condition of the road-bed, and the directness and almost entire absence of curves from that part of the line between St. Gedeon, where Lake St. John is left behind, and Chicoutimi. Between the Hotel Roberval and St. Gedeon, a distance of some twenty-nine miles, the railway skirts the shores of Lake St. John, running around fully one third of its circumference, and affording very magnificent and ever-changing views of the great inland sea. The first fourteen miles of the journey is a return to Chambord Junction, over a section of the railway already described. The new division of the road is equal in every respect to the main line from Quebec to Chambord, and in some respects is superior to it from the very nature of the country through which it runs. Its embankments are exceedingly wide, its bridges are iron and of the very best, and it is laid throughout with steel rails.

Five miles after leaving Chambord and branching off on the new division of the road, the railway crosses the mouth of

The Metabetchouan River,

upon a handsome iron bridge, five hundred feet long, that cost the Company $100,000. Upon the east bank of the river is still to be seen the old fort of the Hudson Bay Company. There are splendid falls a few miles up the river, and at the foot of these, and in the mouth of the stream, excellent ouananiche fishing is to be had in the spring and autumn seasons.

Six miles after crossing the Metabetchouan bridge, and nine from Chambord Junction, the train stops at

St. Jerome,

the centre of an excellent agricultural country, through which the railway runs for many miles, calling at various stations, from which are shipped the produce of some thirty butter and cheese factories. This part of the country consists principally of rolling land that reminds the visitor of the most highly favored portions of the Eastern townships. Frightful forest fires have swept over much of this country. Here and there along the line of the railway may still be seen traces of the awful conflagration of 1870, of which Adirondack Murray says: " The record of forest fires, east and west, might be searched in vain to find a parallel. It was no ordinary fire, but a cyclone of flames, that swept the earth as with the besom of destruction. Before its awful rush the solid forest was swept away as if its mighty trees were driest stubble. . . . In seven hours that awful line of fire had gone 120 miles; then it suddenly stopped, like a tiger glutted with prey. . . . Men, women, and children fled to the lake and plunged in. Not all escaped. Some were caught in the woods; their bones, even, were never found. Some foolishly hid in their cellars; they were roasted alive. A great wooden cross, by the roadside on the lake shore, tells the passer-by today where a group thus met their dreadful death. Some thought the end of the world had come, so dense the smoke and high the fire, which flamed to the very sky, and said their prayers as at the threshold of judgment day. The heat was indescribable. It ate the woods like dry straw. It split the mighty rocks. Cliffs burst open and fell down with the noise of thunder. . . . The fish in the rivers came to the surface as in boiling water. All living things in the path of the flame perished on the instant."

St. Gedeon

is a station six miles beyond St. Jerome, and about a mile from the village of the same name, which is the home of Mr. Joseph Girard, M. P. P., the indefatigable representative of this section of the country in the provincial parliament. Not far from the station the railway crosses La Belle Rivière, which, as its name signifies, is indeed a fine river, and, nearer to its source, traverses a country famous for the large game that may be hunted in its forests. Mr. Wilson, of Denver, Colorado, had splendid sport here in the fall of 1891.

Some six and a half miles beyond St. Gedeon station, and twenty-one and a half from Chambord Junction, the train pulls up at

three or four miles from the village of that name, which is the
largest in the whole Lake St. John country, containing a population of at least 3,000 souls. The parish has several good
country stores, and a stone church that cost $60,000. Hebertville
takes its name from the Rev. Mr. Hebert, a former parish priest
of St. Paschal, in Kamouraska county, who conducted the first
party of settlers to the scene of the present populous parish,
which was then, in 1849, covered with virgin forest. A short
distance to the south are the extremely picturesque lakes, Kenogami and Kenogamichiche, both of them swarming with fish,
and to the north, the new parish of St. Bruno, possessing excellent soil, upon which settlement is making rapid progress, and
connected by an iron bridge, recently erected by government
over the Little Discharge, with the still more northerly parish of
St. Joseph d'Alma on Alma Island. It may be interesting to note
that beyond the Grand Discharge, which washes the northern
shore of the Island of Alma, there are two more newly formed
parishes, laid out upon a portion of the large tract of fine land
bordering upon the lake, between the Grand Discharge and the
Peribonca.

Just east of Hebertville station the railway runs through the
picturesque

Dorval Pass.

This pass is a narrow opening, cleft by some remarkable force
of nature through the mountains, and forms the bed of the little
river Dorval, beside which pretty stream there was barely space
in some localities between the cliffs on either side of the pass to
permit of the construction of the railway. This pass is over a
mile in length, and in and about it some splendid specimens of
iron ore have been found.

Jonquiere Station

is reached at the forty-first mile from Chambord Junction. It is
close to the River aux Sables, where there is quite a flourishing
village. The station is so named after one of the last French
governors of Canada, who ruled from 1749 to 1752, in which latter year he died at Quebec. Here, as at Hebertville, St. Gedeon,
St. Jerome, and elsewhere in the Lake St. John country, is the
centre of a rich, happy, and contented agricultural population,
thriving to their heart's content upon the fertility of the soil and
the result of the profitable dairy industry in which the greater
number of them are engaged. In their own methods of life and

in their religious faith, simple-minded trust, happy contentedness and frugality, they remind the readers of " Evangeline," of the Acadians of the story, while their houses and villages might almost pass for those of Grand Pré, as so inimitably described by Longfellow. The resemblance is particularly marked in these lines : —

" There in the midst of its farms reposed the Acadian village.

＊ ＊ ＊ ＊ ＊ ＊ ＊ ＊ ＊ ＊ ＊ ＊

Solemnly down the street came the parish priest, and the children
Paused in their play to kiss the hand he extended to bless them.

＊ ＊ ＊ ＊ ＊ ＊ ＊ ＊ ＊ ＊ ＊ ＊

. . . . Anon from the belfry
Softly the Angelus sounded, and over the roofs of the village
Columns of pale blue smoke, like clouds of incense ascending,
Rose from a hundred hearths, the homes of peace and contentment.
Thus dwelt together in love these simple Acadian farmers —
Dwelt in the love of God and of man. Alike were they free from
Fear, that reigns with the tyrant, and envy, the vice of republics.
Neither locks had they to their doors, nor bars to their windows ;
But their dwellings were open as day and the hearts of the owners.''

Here, too, are to be seen the thatch-roofed barns, bursting with produce, exactly as sung of the Acadians by the American poet, and if the tourist steps into the interior of the farm-houses in this country he may see the counterpart of Evangeline's picture,

" Spinning flax for the loom, that stood in the corner behind her,"

and spinning it, too, upon the most old-fashioned of spinning-wheels.

The Approach to Chicoutimi

by the railway is magnificently grand. Bursting upon the admiring gaze of the travelers on board the train, four miles before reaching the town, is an ever-to-be-remembered view of the Saguenay, more than three hundred feet below. The scene is truly a beautiful one. There is the picturesque and far-famed water-course stretching away below, and on either hand and in front are the heights of the northern shore, and upon them, just over the river from Chicoutimi, the pretty village of St. Anne du Saguenay. From the point where the railway first overlooks the Saguenay River it runs gradually down to the level of the government wharf at Chicoutimi, with a maximum grade of eighty feet to the mile.

A mile and a quarter from its destination the train crosses a bridge, sixty feet high, over a picturesque ravine, through which the Chicoutimi River rushes to mingle its laughing, leaping waters, by a fall fifty feet high, with those of the River of Death, as Bayard Taylor calls the Saguenay.

The Chicoutimi River rises near Lake Jacques Cartier, in the County of Montmorency, and flows northward into Lake Kenogami, issuing from it again to run an exceedingly rapid course of seventeen miles more, descending in this brief, latter career, no less than 486 feet, by seven falls and a continuous series of rapids. The portage at one of the falls takes its name of " Portage de l'Enfant" from the story of an Indian baby who was left in a canoe that, being carelessly fastened, was carried away by the current, and leaped the fall of fifty feet without upsetting.

Operated by the water of the Chicoutimi River, and situated near by the railway bridge, are

Price's Mills.

These form one of the institutions of Chicoutimi, and one of the largest milling establishments in Canada, furnishing employment to a vast number of men, and through them, and in connection with their other ramifications, sustaining many of the other industries of the place. In fact, the history of the business operations of the Price family is that of the settlement of the Saguenay valley. The head of the house for the time being has for nearly a century borne the title of " King of the Saguenay." The present sovereign of the " *Royaume du Saguenay*," as this territory was called in the first century of French domination of Canada, is Senator Price of Quebec. Mr. William Price, who came to Canada in 1810, was the founder of the house which bears his name, and erected the first lumber mills, both at Chicoutimi and Tadousac. On one of the loftiest points of land in the town of Chicoutimi stands a monument to the memory of his son, the late Mr. William Price, Jr., who died in 1880, after having represented Chicoutimi and Saguenay for some time in parliament. Chicoutimi has a Roman Catholic bishop, Mgr. Labrecque, and a handsome cathedral church and college, built of stone, besides two large convents. A new chapel was erected in the early part of 1893, quite close to Price's mill, upon the site of the little old Jesuit chapel built for the Indians in 1670, and replaced by another erected in 1727 by Father Laure. Michaux, the French botanist who ascended the Saguenay about the end of the last century, described the chapel as being then in a good state of preservation, and constructed of white cedar. In 1850 the remains and site of the old relic were carefully fenced in by Mr. Price. When the foundations were being dug for the new chapel, in November, 1892, the remains of a coffin and human bones were discovered by the workmen beneath the site of the chancel of the old chapel. With these remains were found interred a number of curious relics, including an arrowhead, an iron socket, the point of a sword, plates of metal, and the teeth of bears and beavers, that had apparently been used as ornaments. Conjecture has since been rife as to the identity of the remains, which some people affect to believe must be those either of some missionary to the Indians or of an Indian chieftain or other prominent convert to Christianity.

Magnificent Steamers.

Regular floating palaces are the Saguenay and St. Lawrence River steamers of the Richelieu & Ontario Navigation Company, which connect with the trains of the Quebec & Lake St. John Railway at Chicoutimi. Their extensive promenade decks are admirable for purposes of observation; their staterooms, ladies' cabins, saloons, dining-rooms, etc., are marvels of elegance and comfort, while the *cuisine*, the service of the meals, and the attendance on board leave nothing to be desired. To promote the pleasure and the comfort of the passengers is the constant aim of all the officials of the steamers, from their captains down.

The Saguenay.

At Chicoutimi we are some sixty-eight miles from the mouth of the Saguenay which, nearly as far again to the west of us, takes its rise where the surplus waters of Lake St. John are poured out into the awful chasm where the Laurentian Mountains were wrenched asunder by some violent convulsion of nature. No other river on the face of the earth affords such startling contrasts to the tourist as the Saguenay does. It draws its bright young life from the commingling of its parent streams upon the elevated bed of Lake St. John, and is twinfold in its early infancy, where the prattling and the babbling waters of the newborn river are divided into two streams by the Island of Alma. For the first nine miles of its existence on either side of the isle, it leaps and gambols in frolicsome display, heedless of the rocks that it encounters on its way, now basking in pleasure and sunlight, regardless of the coming night, now flashing, dashing, crashing, in the full vigor of lusty youth, over precipitous declines. After the reunion of the sometime separated waters, at the foot of Alma Island, there is a continuation for thirty to forty miles more of the precipitous cascades, and falls, and rapids, of the utmost violence, until, some few miles above Chicoutimi, the excitement, and life, and elasticity, and unrest of youth give place to the splendid awe and magnificent gloom that settle down upon the adult dark river, becoming deeper and more impressive as they later approach

the stygian darkness of its latter end. A Dante or a Gustave Doré might have created a reputation by depicting the leading features of the Saguenay, either in language or upon canvas.

The lower Saguenay, pouring down towards the sea its dirgeful flood of dark and almost unfathomable waters, along its bed of volcanic origin, cleft between precipitous banks of adamantine rock, attracts yearly an increasing number of that ever-extending class of refined and educated American tourists, whose chief delight it is to read and study Nature for themselves from the most fascinating pages of her ever-open book. One of the most highly cultured and most deeply learned of his class — Mr. W. H. H. Murray — thus describes the birth of the Saguenay : " It is a monstrous cleft opened by earthquake violence for sixty miles, through a landscape of mountains formed of primeval rock. In old time a shock which shook the world burst the Laurentian range asunder at its St. Lawrence line, where Tadousac now is, and opened up a chasm, two miles across, two thousand feet in depth, and sixty miles in length, straight northward. Thus was the Saguenay born."

The present writer was not there at the time to see, and so gladly accepts Mr. Murray's story of the event, especially as it stands corroborated by the most noted geologists of the day.

Professor Roberts says : " The Saguenay can hardly be called a river. It is rather a stupendous chasm, from one to two and one half miles in width, doubtless of earthquake origin, cleft for sixty-five miles through the high Laurentian plateau. Its walls are an almost unbroken line of naked cliffs of syenite and gneiss. Its depth is many hundred feet greater than that of the St. Lawrence ; indeed, if the St. Lawrence were drained dry, all the fleets of the world might float in the abyss of the Saguenay, and yet find anchorage only in a few places."

A writer in the London *Times* calls it " Nature's sarcophagus," and declares that, " compared to it, the Dead Sea is blooming." He continues : " Talk of Lethe or the Styx — they must have been purling brooks compared with this savage river." The Indian name of the river was " Pitchitanichetz."

From Chicoutimi to the entrance of Ha! Ha! Bay, eleven miles down the river, the scenery is bold, indeed, but less gigantically so than that which greets the traveler nearer the mouth of the stream. Almost immediately opposite to Chicoutimi are Cape St. François and the parish of St. Anne du Saguenay. Lower down than these, the little rivers l'Orignal, Caribou, and Outardes flow into the Saguenay. They take their names from the immense numbers of moose, caribou, and wild geese respect-

ively that are hunted and killed along their banks. The parish
below St. Anne rejoices in the musical name of l'Anse au Foin,
or Grass Bay, where a saw-mill affords employment to a large
proportion of the population. The word "Anse" signifies Bay,
and so we have, on the Saguenay river, not only l'Anse au Foins,
but l'Anse St. Jean, l'Anse a la Barque, l'Anse a l'Eau, and a
number of other peculiarly named bays. Another striking name
for one of the Saguenay harbors is "La Descente des Femmes,"
or "the getting-down place for the women." And what a getting
down it must have been there! It is some six or eight miles
below Ha! Ha! Bay, on the opposite side of the river, and is so
called because it was at this point that a number of Indian
women, whose husbands were dying of hunger in the interior of
the country, reached the Saguenay on their way to seek food and
assistance.

Ha! Ha! Bay

is a large inlet seven miles deep, that is supposed to have taken
its name from the laughing exclamations of the first French
navigators of the Saguenay, who, having entered it, thinking that
it was the main channel of the river, or the estuary of some very
large river, found themselves landlocked upon every side. Its
Indian name is Heskuewaska. Its remotest shores are now lined
with the meadows of St. Alphonse. The little rivers Mars and
Ha! Ha! which flow into this bay are noted for their trout and
salmon. Guarding the entrance to Ha! Ha! Bay is the rugged
promontory, Cape West, and immediately opposite to it, on the
other side of the Saguenay, is the equally bold Cape East. The
grandeur of these capes is increased by the narrowing of the
river at this point to some half a mile in width. Cape East rises
almost perpendicularly to a great height above the water, while
about its base are strewn a number of immense granite boulders,
from the interstices between which spring up a number of stunted
trees.

A few miles after passing "La Descente des Femmes," already
described, there looms up before the tourist, on the south shore,
about fifty miles from Tadousac, an enormous rock of singular
form and grandeur, which, at a height of several hundred feet, pre-
sents a perfectly vertical and polished surface, just as if it were a
canvas stretched in readiness to receive a monster picture from
the brush of some aerial artist. Hence it is called "Le Tableau,"
or "the picture." We are now approaching the grandest scenery
of the entire Saguenay trip. Two enormous mountain promontories, on our right as we descend the stream, command our atten-

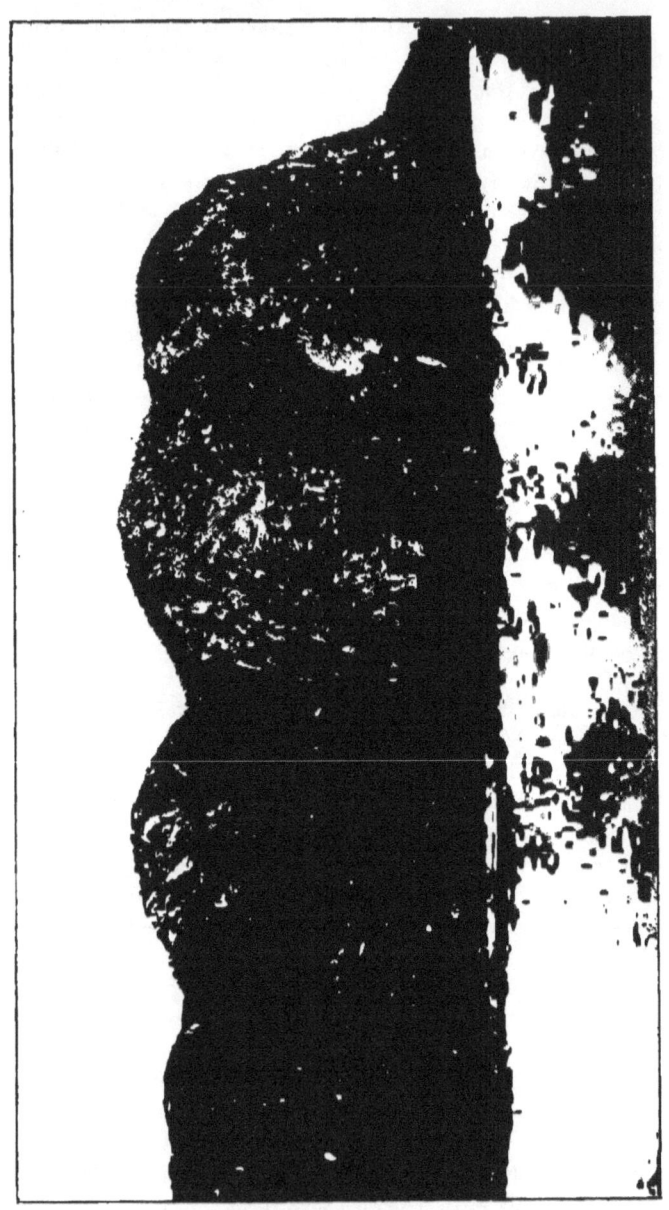

tion for some time before we reach them, by the very boldness
and massiveness of their imposing splendor.

There is an exceptional grandeur, a majestic sublimity about
their very names:

"Trinity" and "Eternity."

Three different elevations, and yet but one rock! Three distinct heights, and yet each about the same in its own individual
extent and proportions! Three equal steps; yet each distinct
from the other; and one great, awful "Trinity" of cape and
mountain raising aloft its summit to a majestically precipitous
height of 1,700 feet! Some pious soul, mindful of the exhortation
of the sweet singer of Israel to "mountains and all hills" to
praise the name of the Triune God, has endeavored to contribute
towards the obeying of the command by planting the symbol of
redemption upon the summit of Cape Trinity. Nobody who
gazes, even for a second, upon this triple-crowned promontory, will
think it necessary to inquire the origin of its name. Nearer and
nearer to its precipitous cliffs glides the steamer, and in proportion as the intervening space grows less, does the true appreciation
of the awful height and massive grandeur of the cape increase.
At last, as the vessel steams around the point and still nearer in
to the adamantine walls of the frowning precipice that seem ready
to fall over upon it, a feeling of awe possesses everybody on deck,
and the contrast between the relative size and apparent importance
of the steamer and all on board of her on the one hand, and of
the natural surroundings on the other, is for the moment overpow-
ering, and for once in his life the tourist is unavoidably confronted
with an enforced reminder of his own utter insignificance.

The immense height of these perpendicular cliffs renders distance deceptive. The steamboat appears to be sailing dangerously
close to the precipice, that looks to be but a few feet distant from
its decks. You pick up a pebble from a bucket standing on the
deck, and think it an easy matter to throw it against the rock. To
your surprise it falls far, very far, short of your aim. The steamer
is now in Eternity Bay, that separates the two great capes; and,
amid the deep solitude of such surroundings, you start affrighted
at the sound of your vessel's whistle, and are impressed beyond
measure by the long-continued and oft-repeated reverberations of
its echo. Nor is your feeling of awe in any way lessened by the
remembrance of the fact that the still, black water of the river out
of which these mountain capes so abruptly rise is nearly 2,000
feet deep. Cape Eternity is more than a hundred feet higher than
Trinity, or nearly six times as high as the Citadel of Quebec, and

if ever mountain anywhere deserved a name signifying that it was
what it is, is what it was, and shall be both what it was and what
it is, that mountain is assuredly Cape Eternity. Yet the knowledge
of what has been, and the belief of what shall be, reminds us that
even this "everlasting hill" is only comparatively so, and the man
of Uz might have had in his mind the birth of the Saguenay when
he wrote, 3,400 years ago, "He overturneth the mountains by the
roots. He cutteth out rivers among the rocks."

From Cape Eternity to Tadousac the scenery is of the most
sublime grandeur. The river is just sufficiently winding and
indented with bays to cause a new panorama of majestic splendor
to open out before the tourist as each successive cape is rounded.
St. John's Bay, or l'Anse St. Jean, is about six miles below
Eternity, and affords good anchorage for ships. A little lower
flows in the Little Saguenay, and on the other side of the river we
pass, half an hour later, the mouth of the Marguerite, a famous
salmon stream, and the principal tributary of the Saguenay. But
just before this come a couple of islands of some two miles each
in length, Isle St. Louis and Isle St. Barthelemy, or Isle Coquart ;
the latter name having been given it in honor of the last Jesuit
missionary but one, who had charge of the Saguenay Indians, and
who died at Chicoutimi in 1765. After the mouth of the Marguerite come St. Etienne Bay, Passe Pierre Islets, and the Point
la Boule, — the latter a towering cape of granite which, as
Professor Roberts remarks, appears for some time to bar our way.
This is but three or four miles from

Tadousac,

and the mouth of the Saguenay. Two rocky promontories guard
the entrance to the dark river, the Pointe aux Bouleaux on our
right hand as we descend, and the Pointe aux Vaches on the left.
The latter was so called after the numbers of the sea-cow or
walrus that are reported to have swarmed here in early times,
where they were hunted by the Basques. Now, as then, large
schools of grampus, a species of whale, may often be seen dis-
porting themselves upon the surface of the water, off the mouth
of the river, while most excellent sea-trout fishing may be had
throughout the summer season in the various coves or bays both
around and within the entrance to the Saguenay. The steamer
usually remains long enough at Tadousac wharf to enable passengers to land and visit the government salmon hatchery which is
close by. There is a large, comfortable, and well-kept summer
hotel here, and near by is the cottage where Lord Dufferin made
his summer home when governor-general of Canada. The name

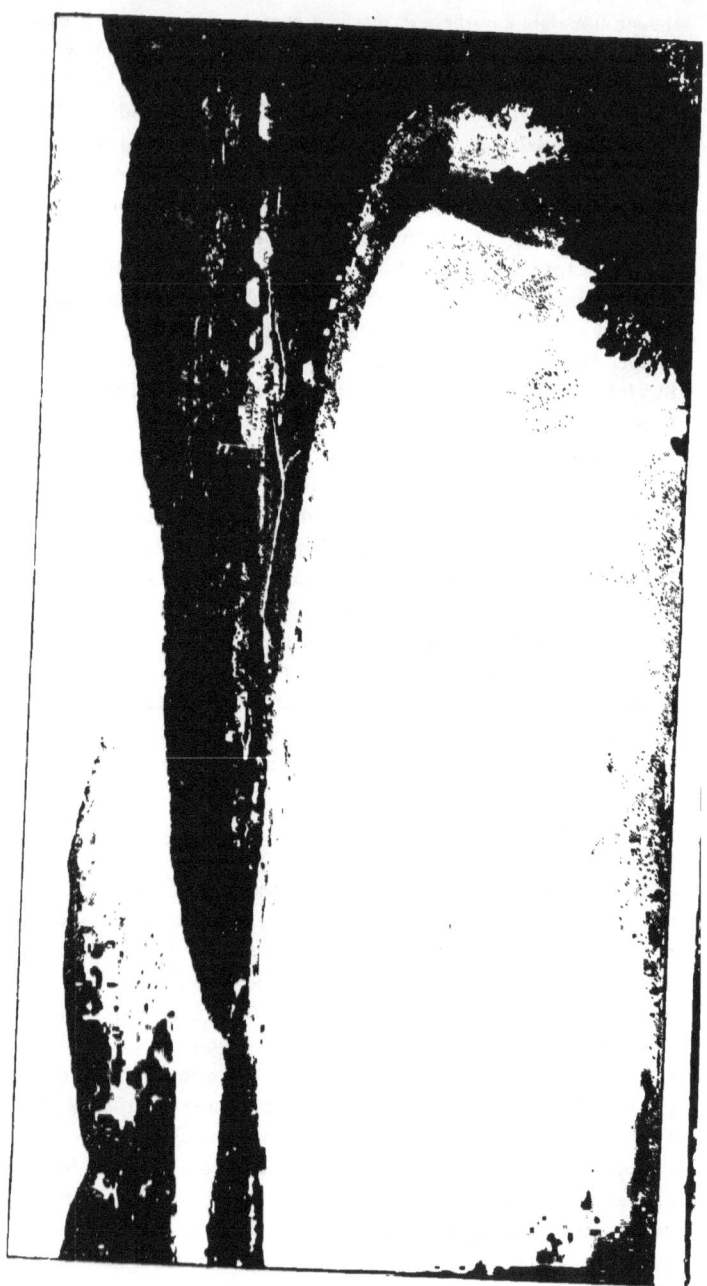

Tadousac, in the Montagnais dialect, signifies "Mamelons," the huge, round hills of sand by which the village is surrounded. According to the Indian missionary, Laflèche, the exact Indian name for Mamelons is "Totoushak." "The Doom of Mamelons" is an entrancing Indian romance by Mr. W. H. H. Murray, the plot of which lies principally in and about Tadousac, and in the interior of the pine-clad, mountainous country that stretches away north of it towards Hudson's Bay. It should be read by all educated and cultured tourists who are interested in Indian lore, and in these huge sand mounds, "which rise in tiers to the height of 1,000 feet or more above the Saguenay, and are supposed to be the geologic beaches of the morning of the world, and to mark in their successive terraces that shrinkage of the waters by which the earth's surface came to view." Tadousac has a marvelous history, having been visited by Jacques Cartier, the discoverer of Canada, in 1535. The Jesuit missionaries had a mission here as early as 1639. Only within comparatively recent years have white men settled permanently at Tadousac, and one of the chief attractions of the place, to this day, is the little old Indian church, built in 1750, on the site of the bark-covered hut which served as a mission chapel until the first church was built in 1648. Our notice of Tadousac cannot be more fitly closed than by the wonderful legend of the last Jesuit missionary who ministered here to the swarthy Montagnais, Père La Brosse, who died in 1782. The Father, so the story runs, had been working hard all day, as usual, among his converts and in the services of the church, and had spent the evening in pleasant converse with some of the officers of the post. Their amazement and incredulity may be imagined when, as he got up to go, he bade them good-bye for eternity, and announced that at midnight he would be a corpse, adding that the bell of his chapel would toll for his passing soul at that hour. He told them that if they did not believe him they could go and see for themselves, but begged them not to touch his body. He bade them fetch Messire Compain, who would be waiting for them next day at the lower end of Isle aux Coudres, to wrap him in his shroud and bury him ; and this they were to do without heeding what the weather should be, for he would answer for the safety of those who undertook the voyage. The little party, astounded, sat, watch in hand, marking the hours pass, till, at the first stroke of midnight, the chapel bell began to toll, and, trembling with fear, they rushed into the church. There, prostrate before the altar, hands joined in prayer, shrouding his face alike from the first glimpse of the valley of the shadow of death, and from the dazzling glory of the waiting angels, lay Père La Brosse, dead. What fear and sorrow must have mingled with the pious hopes and tender prayers of those rough traders and rougher Indians as, awe-stricken, they kept vigil that April night. With sunrise came a violent storm; but mindful of his command and promise, four brave men risked their lives on the water. The lashing waves parted to form a calm path for their canoe, and wondrously soon they were at Isle aux Coudres. There, as had been foretold by Père La Brosse, was M. Compain waiting on the rocks, breviary in hand, and as soon as they were in hearing his shout told them he knew their strange errand; for the night before he had been mysteriously warned; the bell of his church was tolled at midnight by invisible hands, and a voice had told him what had happened and was yet to happen, and had bade him be ready to do his office. In all the missions that Père La Brosse had served, the church bells, it is said, marked that night his dying moment.

To this charming legend the Abbé Casgrain adds: " For many years the Indians going up and down the Saguenay never passed Tadousac without praying in the church where reposed the body of him who had been to them the image of their Heavenly Father. They prostrated themselves with faces to the ground above his tomb, and, placing their mouths at a little opening made in the floor of the choir, they talked to him as in his lifetime, with a confidence that could not fail to touch God's heart. Then they applied their ears to the orifice to hear the saint's answer. In the ingenuousness of their faith and simplicity of their hearts they imagined that the good father heard them in his coffin, that he answered their questions, and afterwards transmitted to God their prayers, This touching custom has ceased since the removal of the remains of Père La Brosse. The abandonment and ruin into which the chapel of Tadousac had fallen decided the removal of these holy relics a good many years ago to the church of Chicoutimi."

From Tadousac the steamer crosses the St. Lawrence diagonally to Rivière du Loup, a distance of some twenty-two miles, passing, as it nears the south shore, immediately in front of

Cacouna,

the most fashionable of Canadian watering-places, which has been frequently termed the Newport of Canada, from the wealth and fashion of its summer guests, who own cottages there or take apartments at the St. Lawrence Hall, the large hostelry owned by Messrs. Shipman & Stocking, that crowns the heights overlooking the great river. It is by far the largest and most popular hotel at any St. Lawrence river resort in Canada, and has accommodation for four hundred guests.

Rivière du Loup is also an important watering-place, and possesses several hotels and quite a number of elegant private cottages. The drive from the steamboat wharf to Cacouna occupies less than half an hour, and is one of the most picturesque in the country. From Rivière du Loup the tourist may either proceed to Quebec, 116 miles distant, by Intercolonial Railway, return to Lake St. John by the steamer that crosses here with his own, or continue on board the latter until it reaches Quebec, which is usually about 6.30 A. M., in which case the pretty and romantic watering-place of Murray Bay will have been reached about ten o'clock at night.

At least a short stay at each of these summer resorts — say at Lake Edward, Roberval, the Grand Discharge, Tadousac, Cacouna, and Murray Bay — is recommended to the tourist or pleasure seeker. At each he will find a comfortable hotel, reasonable terms, and delightful facilities for fishing, bathing, driving, and other amusements. At each, too, will he experience the health-giving effects of a balmy and exhilarating climate, but nowhere more so than at either Roberval or the Grand Discharge. Here, not only is the bracing atmosphere redolent with the resinous odors of the pine and the balsam, but the air of this far northern country is so tempered by the prevalence of so large a body of water, that the months of September and October are here the most comfortable of the year, and have an average temperature at Lake St. John higher than at either Montreal or Quebec. Invalids from quite a number of the American States have been sent by their physicians to Lake St. John, and have derived great benefits from a summer's stay at this great natural sanitarium.

It well repays the tourist to be up and on deck some little time before the steamer arrives at Quebec. Passing the upper end of the Island of Orleans a magnificent view is had of the far-famed Falls of Montmorency on the north shore, while in front looms up a scene of incomparable beauty, a city set upon a hill, regal in the splendor of its commanding situation, and crowned by the world-renowned Citadel fortress. Crowded upon a lower plateau, but still high above the river, — their tin roofs glittering like silver in the morning sun, — are the cathedrals, convents, colleges, and educational institutions which have contributed to Quebec's fame, and to some extent, at least, justify her claim to be the Athens of Canada. Behind the frowning guns of the Grand Battery is the Cardinal's Palace, and, adjoining it, the great university bearing

the name of Monseigneur de Laval, the pious founder of its pare
institution. Within its walls are educated the descendants of tl
old French *noblesse*, who form the aristocracy of French Canad
and who in Parliament, in the Church, and in the British arn
nobly maintain the prestige of the chivalrous nation to whic
they owe their origin.

As the steamer glides to her moorings under the shadow of tl
vast fortification, the student of history will "mark well h(
battlements," and is constrained to recall to memory the mar
stirring events which these walls have witnessed. Now, for ov(
130 years, the bugle notes so dear to the heart of the British re
coat have succeeded to the beat of the French drums, th;
marked the century and a half of Quebec's history preceding tl
eventful campaign of 1759. Only a few hundred yards to tl
west of the Citadel are the heights of Abraham, where the 2d an
3d battalions of the 60th regiment (Royal Americans), share
with the famous 78th Highlanders and other British corps, und(
Wolfe, the honor of the victory that was so stubbornly dispute
by the gallant Royal Roussillon and their equally brave comrade
in-arms of the sister French regiments of Languedoc, La Sar1
and Guienne, under the intrepid but unfortunate Montcalm.

The "Royal American," later the 60th Foot, and now tl
King's Royal Rifles — a corps raised by the American colonists i
1755, and which has since become one of the most distinguishe
in Her Majesty's service — was with the dying Wolfe on th;
memorable occasion when he gave orders to intercept the retre;
of the French army across the River Charles, which forms th
northern boundary of the city of Quebec. By a singular coinc
dence, the River Charles at Boston, which, like its Quebec nam(
sake, forms the northern boundary of a city fairly reveling in th
wealth of its historical associations, was little more than a decac
and a half later crossed by the redcoats, on that eventful day in 177
of which Americans are so proud. And yet another coincidenc
remains to be noted : More than a century after its honorabl
service under Wolfe, this former Boston regiment was the last t
march out of the chain gate of the Citadel when the imperi;
forces were withdrawn from Canada in 1871. The stories of th
two historical cities of the continent are thus strangely linkec
and it is not unworthy of note that it is to Francis Parkman, th
cultured historian of Boston, that Quebec is indebted for th
most picturesque and entrancing delineation of her own romanti
past.

Hardly a stone's throw from the steamboat landing, at the foc
of the precipice upon which stands the Citadel, the brav

Montgomery met his death in 1775. Bordering upon the overhanging Dufferin Terrace is the Governor's Garden, and beneath the shade of its beautiful trees may be discerned the monument erected to the joint memory of the two heroes of Quebec, and bearing the well-known inscription, so touching in its simple, classic beauty, "*Mortem virtus communem, famam historia, monumentum posteritas dedit.*"

Notwithstanding the withdrawal of the Imperial troops, there are still heard from the King's Bastion on the Citadel, resounding

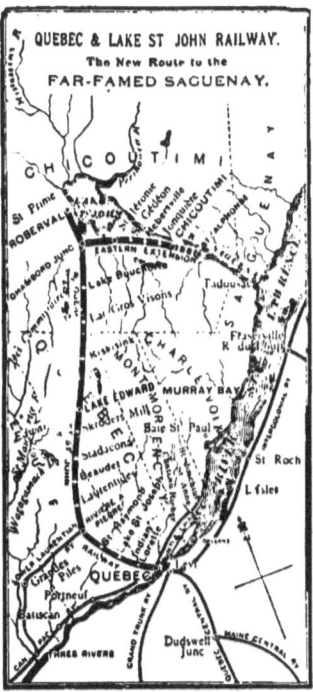

over the ground once trodden by Champlain, Frontenac, Montcalm, De Vaudreuil, Murray, Lord Nelson, and Montgomery, the familiar notes of the bugle calls which bring Tommy Atkins to a sense of his duty, whether he be at Halifax. Bermuda, Gibraltar, Malta, Cairo, Bombay, or distant Burmah ; and from the highest point of the fortress still floats lazily on the summer breeze the red cross of St. George, the emblem of that empire upon which the sun never sets, and which nowhere waves over a land more richly endowed by Nature with all that goes to make up the ideal paradise of the tourist and the sportsman, than that through which we have now drawn our triangular trail.

QUEBEC AND LAKE ST. JOHN RAILWAY.

GENERAL OFFICES:

ST. ANDREW STREET TERMINUS,
(Princess Louise Dock.)

QUEBEC.

FRANK ROSS	President.
E. BEAUDET	1st Vice-President.
S. PETERS	2d Vice-President.
J. G. SCOTT	. Secretary and Manager.
ALEX. HARDY	. Gen'l Passenger Agent.
JOS. ST. ONGE	. Trav. Passenger Agent.
R. M. STOCKING	City Ticket Agent.